R A N C I D

G R A N T   J O L L Y

SPECIAL THANKS

Moira Macdonald, Margaret Higgins,
Charlotte Hamilton, and you, the
reader.

GRANT JOLLY

RANCID

FOR MUM

'Loneliness has followed me my whole
life. Everywhere. In bars, in cars,
sidewalks, stores, everywhere. There's
no escape. I'm God's lonely man...'

-TRAVIS BICKLE

There is a tale, an urban legend if you like, about a demon who walks among us – a seeker of souls. The Seeker looks and acts human, and can walk freely on earth and bask in the daylight. However, only human souls stop him from turning to foul ash in the daylight. He feeds upon us to keep the fire inside from consuming him.

1

I felt as though everyone was staring at me. All eyes on Frank Denver, the wannabe loser. At least that's what I thought. On close inspection, everyone was looking at *everyone*. That's the way these dumb meetings go. We all sit round in a circle feeling sorry for ourselves and 'share' our stories.

After the meetings I go home and get hammered. I'm not sure why I turn up in the first place, but I do. I guess I like to know that I'm not the only loser out there with a drinking problem. I like the noise I suppose,

the sound of other voices. I'm
usually banged up in my flat with
nothing but the sound of my own
thoughts whizzing around in my head.
Sometimes it makes me nauseous.

Twenty-four and already attending
AA for the company, sad or what? Even
though, I continue to try and
convince myself that I don't have a
problem, deep down, I know I do - and
it's serious.

Anyway, the meetings start at
8:00pm and finish at 9:00pm, so it's
not a lot of time out of my busy
schedule of doing nothing. There's
always this one guy called Johnny who
turns up reeking of booze every
single week. At least I have the
decency to turn up drunk with a
packet of Polo mints in my back
pocket.

Sarah, the addictions counsellor is
sweet. I would say she's in her early

thirties and has an amazing pair of legs. She has a lovely complexion and never has to wear make-up. I often fantasise about her. Who am I kidding, what would a girl like that see in a drunk like me?

She walked in and joined the circle of losers.

"Hello, everyone. How are we all doing?" Everyone gave a half-assed 'hello' back.

"Who wants to share first this week?"

This is the moment that everyone dreads. Not because they have to dribble on about how hard their lives are and how the drink helps, but because old Johnny boy is always the first to share. This guy can hardly stand up at the best of times, let alone speak for five minutes without spluttering all over everyone.

Johnny slowly got to his feet, swayed a little and then steadied himself. He was wearing double-denim, you know, the full works, denim jacket accompanied by a dashing pair of stone-wash jeans.

"Ello everywon, am Johnny and am an alkiholik."

The old bastard was out of it, out of the game, out of his fucking mind.

"I had a little much to drink, but am okaaay. Linda left me yesterday, bitch. Probibly bangin a guy with a bigger dick than mine."

Old Johnny started to blubber like a baby, so I helped him sit back down and gave him a little pat on the back and everyone else gave him a sympathetic applause. No wonder Linda left him, whoever she is; he probably made her up in that chicken-fried brain of his.

"Frank, why don't you share with us

tonight, it's been a while."

Sarah was right. I hadn't shared in almost three weeks. I prepared my speech in my head for a moment before clearing my throat.

"My name is Frank Denver and I am an alcoholic. I started drinking heavily when my father passed. I was still a teenager. He got hit by a truck, drunk walking home from the bar. I guess I followed in his footsteps and this is where it has led me."

Sarah was staring right into my eyes, it was kinda creeping me out. I couldn't concentrate. I wondered if she could hear my thoughts and knew what I was going to say next.

"I drink because I get lonely. I drink because it helps me forget and it makes the world seem a little bit brighter. When I am drunk the darkness in my mind is more bearable."

I took a breath,

"I am a writer. The booze also clogs my creativity, which is bad because I am currently working on a new novel. I have already hit a block. Most of all, I block myself and I want to become a better person, a better writer. Thank you."

I sat down and savoured my sympathy applause. I could still hear old Johnny in the background blubbering on about Linda. He cracked open a can of coke and started slurping at it.

I sat there and listened. Soon the voices in the room became muffled and I started daydreaming about all the things that entered my mind; writing, drinking, fucking. What I did not know at that point is that the very next day, my life would change forever.

2

Most of my days consist of: waking up, staring at the nicotine-yellow ceiling and wondering if it will be the last thing I see before I die. I make coffee, adding scotch first, of course. I then continue my routine by making two slices of toast that I forget about and burn, smother in butter to hide the charcoal and then eat only half a slice because it is so revolting. Halfway through my coffee I decide that it is NOT too early for a real tall glass of scotch – then I wonder what the fuck is wrong with me? I continue to drink my beverage anyway, which I know will lead to twelve more and me being plastered to the floor like a fucking tile. Before becoming a floor tile, however, I sit behind my typewriter. I sit there for most of the day, staring at the blank white page in front of me – wishing it could write on itself. I drink an astounding amount which I can't afford and smoke about a thousand cigarettes which I also can't afford. But not on this day. This day was different.

I can remember that summer well. My life changed that hot afternoon in July. You see, I woke up, stared at the yellow ceiling, and after looking at myself in the mirror and noticing I had grown a beard in what felt like over night, I decided to break my depressing routine. I had fifty quid burning a hole in my pocket and decided I should go out to a bar for a change of scenery.

I still started my day with a large coffee with fifty percent of the mug filled with scotch. I pulled on my jeans, they were beginning to look a bit worse for wear. I rustled around in the linen basket for a t-shirt that didn't smell too bad and put it on. I grabbed my notebook and a pen and stuffed them in my back pocket, you know, just in-case a wave of inspiration hit me.

As I was leaving I noticed myself in the mirror; the beard was out of control with a bright tinge of orange to it but it was too late to shave now, I thought, and headed out the door.

It had been so long since I had drunk in a bar like a human and not alone like an animal, I didn't really know where to go. I didn't really care too much if I am honest.

As I walked down the road into civilization, I realised I was beginning to sweat. I needed a scotch

- quick-style. I sucked on a smoke to try and take my mind off the urge for alcohol and started to walk faster.

The heat in the air was dry and I felt as though I had swallowed a jar of sand. When I finally got into town, I could hear music leaking out from a little alley. I poked my head around the corner and then I approached a pub called 'Hangman's Tavern'.

The place looked grubby as hell, three of the four windows had been boarded up and the wood was covered in red spray-paint('Bonzo is a grass!'). I figured I would fit in well in such a shitty place.

The large, heavy wooden door creaked as I pushed it open. I felt like Clint Eastwood entering a saloon in one of those old spaghetti westerns - everyone sitting inside turned and looked at me as though

Jesus-fucking-Christ had just walked
through the damn door.

I stood there for a second,
savouring the smell of stale sweat
and cheap beer. My feet stuck to the
floor as I made my way over to the
bar. I guessed cleanliness was at the
bottom of the list of priorities for
maintaining this shit-hole. I felt
sorry for the old wooden floor and
wondered when was the last time it
had been caressed by a mop and some
hot soapy water.

I was finally at the bar and ready
to order my first cold bruskie. The
guy running the joint was old and
bald. He was so bald I was pretty
sure his skull was going to burst
through the thin skin on his head and
scream hello - it didn't.

Old Baldy looked at me with his
beady teddy-bear eyes,

"I never saw you before."

I could feel a tension in his voice.

"I guess that's because I've never been here before Mr. I've never even heard of this bar."

Baldy rubbed his chin,

"Smart guy, eh? I hope you're not here for trouble because I just don' need it."

Does my ginger beard and outstanding charisma intimidate this little fella, I thought.

"Mr, I try my best to stay outta trouble, I'm just here to wet my whistle like everyone else."

"Well okay then, but the first sign of trouble and you're out, comprende?"

"Sure as shit - Amigo."

Old Baldy let out a sigh,

"What's your poison, stranger?"

I thought for a moment about how all the things I liked in life *were* poison - booze, smokes...love.

"Gimme a Bud and a half of scotch."

Baldy pulled a glass up from under the bar and blew in it. As he pulled back the pump the liquid gold began to flow. I noticed just how badly I needed to quench my thirst. I could feel that white stuff accumulating at the corners of my mouth like cotton.

This guy may have been a little shifty, but he knew how to pour beer. The creamy head was perfect. I hoped in that moment that it would taste as good as it looked, and it was fantastic, smooth and cold; but not too cold, just the way I like it. He then passed me the scotch and I slammed that down in one.

I ordered another, before taking a seat in the corner booth which was empty.

Although Hangman's was rough on the outside and scabby on the inside, I kinda liked it. The seats were a nice burgundy colour and were as comfy as hell. And even though it was a million degrees outside, it was rather cool inside. And the beer was good, not to mention affordable for a bum like me.

I still couldn't understand how I had never seen this place. How could I miss it? It was situated bang in the middle of town. No matter how hard I tried I could not remember for the life of me if I had seen Hangman's on my travels before. I sure as hell knew I had never stopped in for a drink – old Baldy would have remembered me. I let the thought slip from my mind and continued to drink up.

I wondered about my life and all the stupid mistakes I had made. All the people I had hurt. If I am good at one thing, it is feeling sorry for myself. When I was eighteen, I thought I had an amazing writing career ahead of me.

I published my first book one week after my birthday that year. The book was called *Heaven From Below* – it was pretty successful and got my name out there. My fame lasted about a year and that was it – people forgot and soon my novel disappeared from the shelves and slid deep into the pulp graveyard.

For some reason it became hard to write. No matter how hard I tried, I couldn't bash out more than a short story – sometimes a single sentence was a task in itself. My mum left, my dad died from stupidity and before I knew it, I was all alone.

I pulled out my notebook and lay it on the table in front of me with the pen on top. For a second, just touching the notebook gave me a little tingle in my stomach - the

tingle writers get when they know
they are onto a great idea – though
it faded almost instantly. I guess it
may have been faint but I definitely
felt that old familiar feeling.

I had about eight beers and a good
few halves of scotch before the
alcohol began to tell me it was time
to go home. The sun that was beaming
through the window earlier had calmed
and was beginning to set. Baldy
watched me as I got to my feet and
headed for the door.I raised my hand
up to my head and saluted,

"Later, cowboy."

He gave a little snigger,

"Later."

I pulled open the door to the
tavern and escaped into the cooling
summer sun. The stroll home to
nothing was actually quite nice. I
picked up a bottle of scotch and some
smokes on the way home to help me nod

off into darkness.

3

I had terrible nightmares that night.

I was all alone, walking through a forest. I was carrying a typewriter in my left hand. A piece of paper was inserted in the typewriter and it was flapping around in the wind. In my right hand I was gripping a bottle of JB.

The swaying trees towered above me, blocking out the sky. The raindrops entering through the openings in the branches burst on my head and streamed down my face and into my mouth. The drops tasted metallic. I wiped my face and then looked at my hands. My hands were crimson red, for it was not raining water, it was raining blood.

I could hear a humming in the distance, though as it grew closer, it sounded like more of a growl. And as the growl grew closer I could hear the galloping of a horse.

Anxiety began to control me and I panicked. My feet wanted to run, and I decided to let them. As the thundering growl grew closer I veered towards a log cabin up ahead. It wasn't locked and I could enter with haste. I stood as still as I could and tried to control my breathing as I peered through the cracks in the wooden door, out into the dark forest.

There was silence for a moment, and then there was a new sound which I can only describe as electric. The electric sound was followed by a thick blue fog which hovered above the ground and danced up and down and in and out of the trees. It was beautiful for a time and then there was a sudden gut curdling scream; it made my head vibrate and my teeth chatter violently.

There was another brief moment of silence before the Rider approached on a monstrous black horse. The horse had no eyes, only sewn up sockets which were streaming with thick blood.

The rider was dressed from head to toe in green and wore a hooded robe. I could only make out the bottom half of his face. His lips were scarred and his skin looked scaly and dirty.

The horse halted and grunted only a few feet away from the cabin; my heart began to beat faster, so fast that I was terrified the Rider would hear my fear.

He dismounted. His feet were heavy as they crashed down onto the ground, punishing the soil below him. The blue fog was attracted to him and mimicked his every move. I could hear his breathing which scared me as I knew he could also hear mine.

The Rider raised his hand suddenly and pointed directly at me, into the very eye of my soul. My heart dropped to my guts. A foul stench filled the air, the smell of decay. And then he called out with a deep, hoarse roar,

"Come and see!"

At that moment I screamed and awoke in my cold dark room. Alone again, and safe. My body was dripping with sweat and my hair was soaked. I placed my hand on my heart and it was still beating rapidly. I thought it was going to burst free from my chest.

I could still smell the foul stench in the air, and it took me a while to rid it from my nostrils. The dream felt so real and I felt so scared. In that moment of awakening, the only thing I could think about was my father.

The ceiling taunted me as I looked up at it, feeling like a little kid that wanted his mummy to hold him and tell him everything was going to be all right. I then spied the clock on my bedside cabinet and it read 1:00pm. This was the longest I had slept for days, and although I was depressed, I was also feeling strangely optimistic for the first time in ages.

I dragged myself out of bed. My feet welcomed the cold laminate flooring as I stood up. I got dressed, and was soon ready to face another day as a worthless bum. I thought about old Baldy from Hangman's and it made me smile. I guess I could give him another little visit, I thought.

I sat down behind my typewriter in front of the window, fed in a fresh piece of paper. I sat there staring at the blank page; it mocked me, and I guess if it could have spoken one sentence to me it would have been this -

"You know, Frank, you really fucking suck at this game."

Ten minutes passed and I began to feel agitated. The only way I can describe what a 'block' feels like is complete darkness of the mind; no sound, no thought, no nothing. Only darkness and silence. I gave it ten more minutes before heading out the door.

4

By the time I arrived at Hangman's tavern it was almost 2:00pm. As I walked through the front door, Baldy gave me a cheeky little grin and nodded his head to welcome me back. I liked this guy.

I danced along the sticky floor once again and sat on a stool at the bar.

"So, you're back again to 'wet your whistle' I guess?"

"I sure am."

"Bud and a scotch?"

The guy had a good memory.

"Sure thing."

I watched again as the heavenly liquid danced into the glass. As I picked up the beer, Baldy made some more conversation,

"You're the first of the day pal."

I looked around and realised he was right. We were the only two people in the bar.

"Strange."

Baldy let out a sigh,

"It's the damn heat. On days like this, people drink outside in the park or at home in the garden with a big ol' barbecue."

I thought about it for a moment. My father popped into my head again and all I could think about were the summer barbecues he used to do in the backyard when I was young.

"I guess so."

I slung back my whiskey. As I did I realised I didn't even know the bartender's name. I was pretty sure it was far from 'Baldy'.

"Hey, Mr, what's your name?" I asked, reaching out my hand for a handshake.

"Brian Hanger, pleased to meet you...and you?"

"My name is Frank. Frank Denver."

"Well it's nice to meet you Frank, and thanks for your custom. At least I never opened this place up today for jackshit."

"The pleasure is all mine."

I winked at old Brian and headed over to the booth in the corner again. Once more I placed my notebook and pen on the table, hoping for inspiration to overwhelm me.

Today, the place felt different. There was a humidity in the air and the beer tasted a little bit warmer, but I drank it up anyway and still enjoyed it.

I thought about Brian and wondered if he had any family and what else he done with his time other than pulling pints for the people. I thought he

looked as though he would enjoy
watching Formula One racing, you
know, he looked a little bit boring.
Maybe I was wrong. Who knows? Maybe
he was a die hard extreme sports
enthusiast who loved to do naked sky
diving on the weekends when he
clocked off from pulling pints.
Unlikely.

The thought of him falling through
the air with nothing but a parachute
attached to his back, his pecker
flapping about this way and that,
made me laugh a lot inside.

I took my time drinking. I had
nothing to go home for and I was
really starting to like it here. It
was rather peaceful and I was slowly
becoming immune to the dank smell in
the air. I was thinking about asking
Brian if I could mop the floor, free
of charge. I decided against it, just
in case he took offence and barred me

from my new favourite drinking place.

Light entered the empty bar, creeping in like a stalking entity from a distant world, the door creaked. And that was the first time I saw him.

He was tall and thin and entered the bar slowly. His fancy shiny shoes sounded musical as they clapped across the wooden floor; there was a slight echo accompanying his stride.

He looked as though he had just walked away from a funeral; he was wearing a black suit and a white shirt, though his tie was a bright forest green with an embossed flower detail in the same colour. He was wearing a black trilby hat, which I thought was a bit out of the ordinary.

He had the palest, flawless white skin and crystal blue eyes like you had never seen before, set in deep, dark eye sockets.

Long black hair escaped from the back and sides of his hat and it was as smooth as hell. There was something about this man, this stranger; I didn't know what it was at the time, but I could sense it.

Have you ever had that gut instinct about someone who gets on the bus or sits down next to you in a bar, you know, the feeling that something just isn't right? As though you can see through them and see the darkness inside? Well, that is the very feeling I had when he entered Hangman's tavern.

Brian tilted his head as though to greet him. They obviously knew each other. Without a word Brian poured him a vodka and lemonade then added a slice of lemon and a slice of lime. The man walked away without paying.

He sat down at a table just in

front of me to the left. He didn't acknowledge me at first, though I couldn't take my eyes off him. From the inside of his jacket pocket, he pulled out what appeared to be a steel straw and a red handkerchief.

He wiped down the metal straw with the handkerchief before placing it in his drink. He then lay the hanky down on the table and smoothed it out with his hand. He had skinny, bony fingers with long yellow nails.

This guy was strange, any fool could have told you that by just looking at him. I mean, who the hell produces their own straw in a bar, let alone a metal one?

He sucked his drink down in one go then pulled out the lemon and lime, placing them together in a citrus sandwich, sucking out the juice until the fruit was dry and placing the peel back into the empty glass.

I had finished my drink and had to take a leak. I left my notebook at the table, who the hell would steal a notebook, anyway? I headed into the bathroom.

There were two urinals, a dump-stall and a sink, all of which were yellow and disintegrating into nothing. After I had pissed I washed my hands with only water as there was no soap. I wondered if it would have been more hygienic to not wash my hands. And I was probably right. I dried my hands on some rough recycled paper towels and headed back into the lounge.

I ordered another drink, though this time I got two Buds and a double scotch to save me getting up in five minutes, this way I would create more drinking time.

I carried my drinks back to the table and sat down. Something was different. I felt as though something was missing, and as I looked up, I noticed the strange guy with the green tie had his sniffer in my notebook. I thought for a few moments about how I would address this situation.

I looked over at him and coughed. He raised his eyes and peered at me for a few cold seconds before removing his snout and fully acknowledging me. I swallowed, I had no words in me, my mouth was full of alphabet slush. The guy finally started the conversation for me,

"I guess you want this back?"

I was expecting a rough, hoarse voice; like the voice of someone who smokes a hundred cigarettes a day, you know, like Bob Dylan - it wasn't. His voice was very smooth and strangely entrancing.

"Well, it is mine...so, yeah, I

guess I would like it back."

The man smiled, revealing his perfect pearly white choppers. I envied his outstanding smile in that moment and made a mental note that I should get the hole in my left molar fixed, pronto.

"You do realise, son, that most of these pages are empty, give or take a few strange doodles?"

I paused for a moment before replying. I felt like a nervous kid in the playground, just before his first kiss from the girl he'd had a crush on for a whole two weeks.

"Yeah, I know. It is mine after all."

"That it is, kid, that it is indeed. Though why carry around a notebook that you don't write in? Seems a little odd doncha think?"

He was mocking me.

"Well, Mr, it's a terribly long

story. I'm sure you don't have time for it."

"I have all the time in the world, kid. Literally."

He stood and walked over to my table and sat down next to me. He closed my notebook, laid it down on the table and placed the pen on top neatly. He turned and looked at Brian, and a minute later there was a drink being brought over to the table and the ritual with the straw and the handkerchief began all over again.

Who is this man? I thought. But mostly, I wondered what the hell he wanted and what his sudden interest was in me and my near-empty fucking notebook.

He finished his drink in one, with yet another swift slurp through the straw. I then watched as he drained the life out of the poor fruit in his glass. He then continued to engage in conversation with me, which made me a little nervous.

"What's your name anyway, kid?

He reached out his hand as an offering of politeness, and shook my hand as I said -

"My name is Frank."

"I am Calder Gunn, two N's. Some people drop the Calder and call me Gunn, but you can call me whatever you so please, Frankie."

I didn't know where this was leading, but I gave Calder Gunn the benefit of the doubt.

"Are you from around here, Mr Gunn?"

"In a way, yes. I come from everywhere. I'm kind of a lone ranger, a drifter of sorts."

"I know the feeling, believe me."

"I'm actually in town on account of some business, Frankie."

"And what business is that, Mr

Gunn, if you don't mind me asking?"

His eyes narrowed, and he looked through me for a second and then grinned.

"I'm in the business of helping people."

"What kind of people?"

Gunn's grin widened,

"People like you, Frankie my boy."

I could feel the hairs on the back of my neck stand up.

"What does that mean, exactly?"

Gunn patted me on the shoulder and laughed.

"I'm going to get us some drinks and then you can tell me all about this terribly long story of yours."

This guy wasn't leaving, and I feared I was going to have to tell him the story of my success in becoming a failure. He may have been quirky and downright weird, but there was something captivating about him, and to be honest, someone to talk to is far better than no one to talk to. I prepared the speech in my head.

As Gunn made his way to the bar, Brian walked over to serve him. They were whispering, but I could not hear exactly what was being said. Brian was leaning forward and speaking into Gunn's ear. Both of them kept looking over at me. It made me a little uneasy, though I figured it had nothing to do with me.

Soon, Gunn came back to his seat. He brought with him a litre of JB and a bottle of Absolut vodka. I asked him how much for the whiskey and he declined my money.

There is nothing I like more in this world than free drinks, on the house, halle-fucking-lujah! I was beginning to like this Calder Gunn fella. I was beginning to like him a lot. So, we got into it and began to chew the fat.

Gunn pawed my notebook once again,fanning through the pages with his skeletal thumb.

"So, what's the story, Frankie?"

"That's just it, Mr Gunn, there is no story. No matter how damn hard I try, there is no story."

Saying those words out loud made me feel sad as hell. And I realised at that moment just how big a failure I was, and that I would do anything to change it. Just to feel something, to hear the voices of characters in my head would make me whole and give my life purpose again.

"From that, I'm guessing you are a writer? And you have hit some invisible, mental brick wall? Am I right?

I smiled.

"Spot on, Mr Gunn. It's ruining my fucking life. I wake up every single morning and sit there, staring at a blank page, wishing for something to change, a story to pop into my head, an idea, a plot, at least a sentence. And there is nothing, not one morsel of imagination left in this stupid head of mine."

Calder was nodding his head on my every word.

"I can imagine that must be quite frustrating for you, Frank."

"Frustrating is an understatement, it really is."

I was slinging the whiskey back fast and hard and it was beginning to hit me good. I slapped a cigarette in my mouth and sucked on it. A cloud of smoke danced around our booth, it was beautiful. I felt relieved. Getting all the shit out of my head once and for all really made me feel good.

"Can I ask you one question, Frankie?"

"Yeah, sure, fire away."

Gunn paused and his crystal eyes seemed to widen for a moment. He looked excited.

"What would you do to change it?"

I didn't think before I replied,

"Anything."

Gunn exposed his brilliant smile once again,

"Anything?"

"That's what I said. I would do anything to get my life back, to be able to write again."

"I can help you, Frankie my boy...if you want me to."

"How can you help me?

"You have to ask me for help first, Frank."

"Why? What does it matter?"

"It's just the way it works."

I was halfway drunk at that moment, though I can still remember now, thinking it was a strange question to be asking a young man you had just met. Though as I said, I was nearly hammered and replied without thinking. I really wish I hadn't.

"Okay then."

Gunn was staring right into my eyes, with that same look of excitement on his face.

"Mr Calder Gunn, can you please help me?"

"Indeed I can, Frankie. I can make you anyone you want to be. I can give you the talent you dream of. I can do anything you imagine. Most of all, I can fix you."

I began to laugh, for a moment Calder looked offended by my laughter, though he soon joined in, drowning out my laugh with his louder, deeper bellow.

"And how do you suppose you can help me? Do you think you are God or something?"

Gunn raised his eyebrows at the mention of God.

"I know I am not God, quite the opposite actually. I can make an immediate change in your life if you so wish. All you have to do is promise me something in return and you get your life back and more. Simple."

"And what do you want in return? If it's money, I have none. I'm surviving off damn royalty cheques, which, may I add, are getting thin as shit"

"No, not money. Nothing at the moment actually, though if I need something you will give it to me? You said you would do anything after all, did you not?"

I was not sure what this 'something' was, but I rolled with it.

"Okay, I promise to keep to my end

---

of the deal."

Gunn looked like a child who had just been handed the best games console on the market. He reached out his bony fingers once again and shook my hand.

"Deal!"
He exclaimed.

"There is just one thing you have to do right now in order for this to work."

I thought in that moment he was going to pull my brain right out of my head, produce some funky wires from his arse and reboot me. He didn't quite do that. He did however reach into his inside pocket and produce a small silver hip-flask; it had his name inscribed on the front, 'CALDER GUNN'.

"You have to drink from this flask and then the deal is sealed."

"What's in it?"

"Dreams!"

I thought about it. A guy walks into the bar, tells me he can change my life in an instant and I am supposed to drink some shit from his flask; dreams apparently? I was a little cautious but I was also a little curious.

If he was telling the truth, which I doubted, I would have the perfect life, right? But if he was full of shit, which I was sure he was, what would be the harm? I figured he was trying to wind me up so I foolishly played along.

He opened the cap of the flask. The smell of mulled wine escaped and I thought about how my father used to brew his own at Christmas.

I took the flask from his hand, and as he watched, I took a large gulp. Believe me, the stuff may have smelled like mulled wine, but it tasted nothing like it.

It was thick and tasted like petrol. I could feel it sliding down my body and my insides began to burn. The world turned fuzzy. There were now three Calder Gunns in front of me spinning around, laughing that deep laugh of his, thrice. The burning was really starting to *burn*.

What was happening to me? I was scared and I guessed he had spiked the flask with something. I'm going to be raped in a bush, I can remember thinking. Luckily for me, this was not Gunn's intention.

I stood and made my way to the shit-house. Three Brians behind the bar also laughed at me as I stumbled into the bathroom. Everything sounded high-pitched and chipmunk-like, the way DJs make their records sound cheap and nasty.

All I could think about was the

burning inside my belly, it was the most painful thing I have ever experienced in my life. I gripped the sink as the world began to disappear, for a brief moment all I could see was white, and then there was nothing, only darkness.

5

The dreams I had were like nothing I have ever experienced. I kept seeing shapes and bright colours, it felt like a migraine, though more lucid.

My eyes burst open and I felt as though I had been hit in the chest with one of those adrenaline needles. My heart was beating so fast I was scared I was going to use all my beats up in one minute and croak it. I felt as though there was a tiny army in my head, banging away at the inside of my skull with a thousand miniature hammers.

I was breathing in and out like crazy, fighting for air. The feeling of relief to see that I was back in my own shitty house, sweating like a pig in my own shitty bed was terrific.

The first thing I saw when I opened my eyes was the nicotine-yellow ceiling, spinning above my head. Everything seemed more vivid. The pains in my gut were excruciating. I gave a thought for all the women out there who have to put up with this crap every single month. I then made a mental note to never make a single menstruation joke in the future.

What happened last-night?

The last thing I could remember was talking to Calder Gunn. When I said his name aloud, it all started to come back to me. The guy was crazy, I thought. Then I remembered our strange conversation. I really had to strain my brain to remember what exactly we talked about.

What was in the flask? I thought. I settled on the idea that it may have been absinthe and that this Gunn guy was just fooling around with me. I had only ever drunk absinthe once before and the morning-after-symptoms were similar to the cramps I was experiencing.

I am a greedy alcoholic and I am extremely weak when it comes to drinking. I would probably drink my own piss if it came to it and I guess when I was offered a sweet smelling drink from a fancy hip-flask, I just couldn't resist. What can you do?

In my book the only people worse than alcoholics are skin-popping-skagheads. They clog up the streets, begging for change to fulfil their vile addiction. They mug people, they rob houses, they shoplift and it sickens me. These cockroaches don't spare a thought for the carnage they leave behind, for the lives they ruin. The only thing important in life to them is powder in a bag. But who am I to judge?

I realised I had to calm down before I worked myself up to a heart attack. As I lay in my bed I tried to take my mind somewhere else. I began to think about the sun setting in July and the fantastic sound of crisp autumn leaves crunching under my feet. And then my mother and father entered my mind.

I thought about them when I was young, and how they were so madly in love. They used to tell each other every single day, without fail. They used to hold hands and take long walks in the park with not a care in the world. I tried to think about the beautiful paintings my mother used to do on Sunday afternoons, when it was raining outside, and then I began to remember the bad things.

I thought about how they slowly stopped holding hands and how they stopped declaring their love for each other. It all became so bitter in the end, my mum leaving and my dad dying of stupidity.

My eyes began to fill with tears and before I knew it there was a stream of salty water rolling down my cheeks and into my mouth – I needed a drink. Little did I know at that point, I was going to be severely disappointed.

I got out of bed and made my way to the kitchen. I hadn't time for a glass and all that bullshit. I grabbed a bottle of whiskey from the kitchen cupboard and cracked it open. I greedily drank as much of that straight whiskey as I possibly could in one go. The fucked up thing was, I couldn't taste it.

No matter how much I chugged the
bottle, I couldn't taste a thing. It
was as though my taste buds were
numb. Sometimes when I get a
migraine, I lose my sense of taste
and my tongue goes fuzzy. Maybe I
actually did have a migraine in my
sleep, I thought...

And it was just about then that I
felt the sudden urge to write.

I took my bottle of whiskey with me
as I quickly made my way over to the
typewriter. I sat down in my brown
leather chair; today it felt
different, somehow more comfortable.
I inserted a fresh piece of paper
into the Olivetti Lettera 22 and she
came alive almost immediately.

My fingers bounced around the keys
rapidly. I didn't know what the hell
I was writing, but I was *writing*. The
words filled the page quicker than
ever before and soon I had to feed my

baby another piece of the old A4. She was back and she was chewing up paper hungrily.

I sat there in nothing but my underwear and a pair of my father's old sheepskin slippers. My skin was beginning to stick to the leather chair. I lost track of time. I didn't care.

I laughed. I cried. I just couldn't stop typing. The whole world seemed to be silent. The only thing I could hear was the sound of the keys banging ink into the paper in front of me as I assaulted them. It was beautiful, fucking beautiful.

The pile of paper continued to grow on the table next to me. Paper filled with words, glorious rows of wonderful words. The alphabet slush had turned to solid ice and I could only pray that it would never melt.

I never stopped. Even when I was

slugging away the whiskey, I continued to unleash the fury of my mind with one hand. I also sucked on cigarettes, hands free. Smoke danced up my face and stung my eyes, I couldn't have cared less. I was fucking unstoppable.

I had sat there all day long, bashing out lustrous words. Drinking, smoking, writing. It was wonderful, absolutely wonderful. The day began to turn to night and darkness began to steal the light from the room. And it was just then, as I reached for the whiskey with my left hand, I realised the bottle was empty. The crazy thing was, I was nowhere near to drunk. After a full litre of the good stuff, I was stone cold sober.

And then I realised, I hadn't even felt the need to urinate all day long. I hadn't eaten a single morsel, yet I was not hungry. I felt revitalised, fresh as a fucking daisy.

To be honest, in that moment, if Sylvester Stallone had knocked at my door and invited himself in for a coffee, I would have thought nothing of it. And then I remembered what Calder Gunn had said to me. His voice in my head was so clear that I thought he was in the room with me.

To this day I still can't shift these words from my mind,

"I can make you anyone you want to be. I can give you the talent you dream of. I can do anything you imagine. Most of all, I can fix you."

These will be the last words in my mind when I die, and they will probably haunt me for eternity in the afterlife, if I make it there, of course.

I'm pretty sure I am going straight to hell for what I did in the days after my encounter with Mr Calder-fucking-Gunn.

6

The morning sun woke me. I was slumped over my typewriter. As I looked to my left I remembered my writing frenzy. There were around two hundred pages piled next to me. I had written a short novel in just one day. The top page was titled 'When the Magpies Call'. I didn't even know what it was about.

All I could remember was writing it. I felt as though something had taken control of my body and mind and written the story for me. I was exhilarated, fresh and ready for more.

Is this the work of a higher power? I thought.

I stood up and headed into the

bathroom for a shower. I got the shock of my life when I saw myself in the mirror. What I was seeing in front of me was not possible, well, not in this world anyway.

I was twenty-four, though I looked a lot older. I guess it was all the years of stress and failure, not to mention all the self abuse; drinking and smoking. Crows' feet were beginning to appear around my eyes, they were faint, but they were there.

However on that day, as I looked in the mirror, I was no longer *me*. The crows' feet had vanished and my beard was gone. How was that possible? I doubt someone shaved me when I was sleeping and I couldn't remember doing it myself. I couldn't remember shaving because I never did. I had spent the whole day sitting at my typewriter unleashing the fury, remember?

I looked smart as hell. My eyes had a glow in them, a new lease of life; they looked younger and brighter. My skin was fresh and smooth, and then I smiled. My teeth were perfect.

I started to doubt myself. Did my teeth always look this good? Did I always look like this? Everything in my heart at that point told me that this was all down to Gunn. I needed to talk to him. I was losing my fucking mind. I couldn't tell what was real and what was fantasy. Was this all part of the depression, my terrible affliction? Was I still dreaming? Would I wake up in a few minutes in a puddle of my own sweat? Unfortunately, I didn't ever wake up from a dream, for this was my reality.

To summarise: I could no longer get drunk or taste alcohol, I was writing like a prolific madman, my beard had shaved itself, I looked younger, and now I had the fantastic smile I always wanted.

It was all too good to be true, but it was happening right in front of me. I was walking, talking, breathing proof that miracles do exist. At a price, as I would soon find out.

I couldn't stop thinking about Calder Gunn, however, so I got showered and dressed as quickly as I could and stormed out.

I once watched an old film called 'The Art of Dying'. It concerns this stuck up rich guy who is nasty to everyone he meets. All he cares about is making money and spending it. He neglects his wife, while she despises him and only sticks around for the financial security.

So the story goes, the rich guy wakes up in the street. All of his riches are gone, his wife is gone, he

has nothing, not even a home. The
beauty of the story is that he has no
recollection of anything. He just
goes to bed rich and wakes up poor
and gets on with his life with no
memory of what he once had and the
power he once possessed.

This was exactly how I felt, like
the guy in the film, but in reverse.

I had been walking for about thirty
minutes and was finally in town, but
I could not remember where Hangman's
Tavern was exactly. I searched and
searched, but I couldn't find it for
the life of me. I walked down all the
little back streets. I couldn't find
the pub.

I was beginning to get really
agitated and angry. I lit a smoke and
sucked on it. After a few minutes, I
remembered walking into a little
alley, just off the main street. I
finally found it and that's about

when my heart fell to the floor. And bounced back up again.

Hangman's Tavern was closed for business, and had been for years by the looks of things. The whole place was boarded up, the door, all of the windows. The slates on the roof were covered with moss, as was the sign running along the top of the small building. The little pub looked as though it would crash to the ground if you so much as sneezed on it.

I was scared and confused. Was I really losing my mind?

There was a café called 'Bella's' attached to the left-hand side of the tavern which *was* open for business. I decided to go in and ask questions.

The smell of grease and sizzling bacon made me feel queasy as I walked into Bella's. There was a short fat woman with curly grey hair, cooking it up behind the counter. She noticed me walking in and came over.

"What can I get you, love?"

I hate when people call me that. I cringed inside and replied,

"Well, nothing actually."

"If you don't want to order, why did you come in?"

She looked confused, but I don't blame her. I probably looked sketchy as hell.

"I was wondering if I could ask you something?"

"And what would that be?"
I pointed to my right and said,

"I was wondering about the place next door, you know, Hangman's Tavern."

The woman looked even more confused now.

"That old dump! Drives away business. They should demolish it."

"Can I ask you how long it's been closed down?"

"Ha, are you for real? It's been nearly seven years now."

The world began to spin, this greasy shit-hole was making me feel even worse and I felt as though I was going to spew chunks right there on the floor.

"Are you sure?"

The woman looked at me as though I was a fucking mad man.

"I don't know what you have been smoking, son, but I have worked here long enough to remember it being closed down."

There was now a small queue forming behind me.

"But I -"

"Look, if you are not buying anything, please leave!"

This old bag had a bit of bite in her yet. The other customers were looking at me as though I had the plague. I knew the look. For some reason I seemed to get it all the time, you know, people looking down their noses, thinking they are better than you are. Most of the time they are right, too.

"Your cooking smells like shit!"

I said, then staggered out the door of the old grease-house. What was happening to me? How could I remember being in Hangman's if it wasn't even open for business? Was I going insane? Anxiety took hold of me and I hurried home as fast as I could.

I needed to talk to someone, I needed to talk to Calder Gunn. The only thing I could think of was the stuff he had given me to drink the night before, it must have fucked me up. I couldn't even think straight, not in this heat.

Where would I find him? Did he even exist, I thought, or did I imagine him? So many ideas buzzed around in my head, as if my brain was a flower and thoughts were bees. I had to find Gunn. I didn't know then, that he would actually be the one who found me.

7

When I got home, I suddenly wanted to
leave again. I felt claustrophobic,
trapped and utterly confused, to the
point I thought my brains were going
to explode out of my ears. I couldn't
even get drunk, for I would have
climbed inside the bottle and stayed
there until everything had sorted
itself out. My luck was rotten.

I stood there in my kitchen and
smoked about a hundred cigarettes,
trying to figure out the situation.
The small room was so full of smoke I
could hardly see. As disgusting as
that may have been, it comforted me
and I began to feel a little calmer.
My plan then became clear in my head.

I would visit the tavern, break-in

and make sure it was the right place, the place where I had met Calder Gunn and drunk away my sorrows. After all, I was a mess and my head was all over the joint. I could have mistaken the boarded up pub for Hangman's. Maybe I just took a wrong turn somewhere. I hoped.

The day was too young for the old breaking-and-entering. I waited until I had the darkness in my favour. In the meantime I would write, and smoke to soothe my soul. I sat down at my beloved typewriter and began to type, the sound of the keys like music to my ears.

I still smoked like a chimney, but the urge for alcohol had left me. The smell of it made me feel sick, and in a way that made me sad – we had been through a lot, me and the bottle I mean. I guessed my life would be prolonged at least five years, now that I was sober and all.

I was writing for a couple of hours before the sun started to fall in the sky. It was time to go, though I needed to find the appropriate gear for the task. I pulled on some black jeans and a black hooded zipper. I popped a small LED torch into my pocket. I also needed some sort of tool to rip the boards off the windows. All I could find was a claw hammer. I slid it down the back of my jeans then headed out the door and by the time I had walked into town, night was upon me.

As I walked, I thought about my dad and how the drink had ultimately killed him. I realised alcohol had also gotten me into a lot of trouble in the past, not to mention this mess. In that moment, I forgave him for leaving me behind. I actually felt guilty for all the years I had been bitter about his death. From then on I stopped saying he had died from stupidity. Life is too short to hold a grudge, believe me, especially if your beef is with a dead guy.

Anyway, it was dark and I was standing outside the desolate bar, with my hood pulled up, looking like a real creep. I pulled out the hammer and jammed it under a panel of wood covering the window. The wood was already rotten, which made my job a little easier. I ripped off the panel with one swift tug and it fell to the ground with a bang, an echo bounced off the walls and then died.

I stood still for a moment, just until it was quiet again. The window behind the wood was smashed. Other than the jagged edges around the frame, I had a clear entrance. I slid the hammer back down my jeans and climbed up onto the window ledge.

I obviously wasn't cut out to be a burglar for I snagged my ankle on the jagged glass. I could feel the blood trickling down onto the top of my foot – I had no time to care about my injury and jumped down from the window ledge and into the tavern.

The place was as dusty as hell, the air inside was thick and dried out my mouth. I pulled out my torch and clicked it on. I aimed the beam in the direction of the bar, and there it was. This was definitely the place, I could almost see Brian standing behind the bar pulling me a pint. Was that bastard in on this? I thought.

I then sent the beam over to the corner booth. The burgundy seats were still there, and I could vividly remember sitting at the table. I was expecting an old projector to pipe up and show me myself sitting there, like in the horror movies - it didn't, thank Christ. The only thing different about the tavern was the fact that it was full of grime, beyond dirty.

There I was, standing in a magical tavern when I heard the sound of voices coming down the alley. I turned off the torch and waited there in the darkness, standing as still as I could. The voices grew louder and louder. Closed for business, keep on walking, I thought.

The voices finally passed the window and then faded away into the distance and then I was all alone again. I was terrified. There is no way I could explain what was happening to me, I felt vulnerable, as though I was losing control of my life, my mind.

I peered out of the window, making sure the coast was clear, and then

jumped out of the tavern. I was empty
inside, I wished it would all stop,
all go back to the way it was before,
but it didn't — it only got worse.

I got home that night, feeling
exhausted. As I put the key in the
front door and twisted it, my stomach
also turned. My gut told me that
someone had been there, I could sense
it. I could almost see them creeping
around my house in my mind's eye.

I entered cautiously. There was a
familiar smell floating around the
hallway, it stuck to my skin as I
made my way into the lounge.
Everything looked intact. I had not
been robbed for my riches - a dirty
laundry basket full of musty clothes
and an empty fridge-freezer full of
ice. There was something. Someone had
been in my house and left me a
present. It was sitting next to the

Olivetti. My heart skipped a thousand beats.

It looked delightful, a lot of effort had gone into its presentation. A bit bigger than a ring box you would find at a jewellers, it was wrapped in black shiny paper and finished off with a red satin bow.

Maybe there's some kind of sugary treat inside, I thought. I knew it sure as hell wasn't an early birthday present. My mum's soft voice entered my head at that point. She always used to say, 'good things come in small packages'. Somehow, I had the feeling that this parcel could be filled with evil.

I unwrapped it slowly, half sure it was a miniature nail bomb sent to me from the land of the leprechauns, and I guessed it would shred my face into pieces in just a second – it didn't.

There was nothing alarming inside, just a fortune cookie laying there. I was bamboozled. It soon made sense after I cracked it open, it was fragile and crumbled in my hand. There was a piece of paper inside. Looks like I got my sugary treat after all, I thought.

I unravelled the paper coil. *00:04*

your dear friend, CG. I swallowed the crab apple in my throat. Calder Gunn had been here, in my house, which meant he knew where I lived. Was I supposed to be scared? I was. But I wanted to find him and ask him questions, I was nervous as hell.

I knew the note was from Gunn, and I knew the numbers were a time. I took a stab in the dark and guessed I was supposed to meet him somewhere at this time, but where?

The only place I had ever seen him was at the tavern and it was now, how shall I put it, closed for business until further notice. The time was 1:07am anyway, which meant I would have to wait until the next night.

All that was happening in my life at that point started the day I met Gunn. I was pretty sure I was going crazy, so I started to think like a crazy person. What if everything Gunn had said was true? It would mean Gunn had given me back the ability to write, amongst other things.

This also meant we had a deal, did it not? And then I realised we *did* have a deal and there was only one explanation – it was time for me to hold my end of the bargain and give Gunn something in return for the gift he had so blessed me with.

My hands had been twitching all day and it was beginning to get worse. They wanted to write, so I let them. I brushed the crumbs from my hands

and placed the paper coil in my
pocket. I had a thought just then –
how on earth did Gunn get a
personalised message inside the
cookie?

I was content that it was not as
weird as everything else that was
going on, and let the thought slip
away. I didn't have time to worry
about such little things.

I sat down in my comfortable chair
and once again, my hands began to
bounce around the keys of the
typewriter, only this time, my hands
were moving so fast they were a blur.
Everything filtered out of my mind
and I slipped into a deep trance,
concentrating only on the wonderful
feeling of indulging in my own craft.

A good few hours and about a
hundred or so pages of the old A4
later, my hands began to slow down
and I started to come out of the

trance, returning to my dark reality.
I was exhausted, so I went to bed. I
fell asleep as soon as my head hit
the pillow. There were no dreams that
night, nothing.

8

Night had descended once again and it was becoming chilly outside. The wonderful autumn days were ever closer. I pulled on a black denim jacket to keep me from the cold before heading out to meet Calder. I was sick twice before I left. My stomach ached. I was beginning to sweat and my hands trembled. I was sure I was too young for Parkinson's disease.

The cool night air was actually a nice treat, and as I strolled alone in the darkness, the beads of sweat on my forehead became sticky before evaporating completely. This road into town was creepy at night, anxiety began to take hold of me.

I walked down the alley and stood outside the tavern. I assumed this was the meeting place. There was no sign of anyone, no Calder, nobody. I stood there for a while, and as I was about to give up, I heard a growling sound pass through my ears with the breeze. I had heard this sound before. In my nightmares. Had Calder Gunn infiltrated my mind when I was sleeping? Was he the horseman in the forest? I could only hope not.

"Come and see!"

The growling became louder as it got closer, then suddenly the sound was mute and I heard footsteps behind me, clapping down the alley. I turned around, and there he was. Same clothes, the green tie flapping on his chest, same big eyes, a smile to die for. My first instinct was to run. I decided against it. My feet would have stuck to the street like glue if I tried, just to piss me off in my moment of need.

He drew closer towards me. Smiling. I tried to smile back, I probably looked as though I had overdosed on botox. Gunn could smell my fear and he liked it. After a moment he was right there in front of me. He reached out his hand, I felt obliged to shake it.

"Frankie, my boy! Long time no see,"
he exclaimed.

I acted as calmly as I could on the outside, though I was literally melting away on the inside, like an ice-cream sundae in a 1000 watt microwave. I thought I was a good enough actor to keep up the front. I replied without spraying Gunn with slush,

"Mr. Gunn..."

"Look, you can relax, kid, I'm not

here to hurt you."

He placed his hand on my right
shoulder and I instantly felt at
ease, as though he had put some
fucking voodoo spell on me. The first
thing that popped into my head after
that was the fortune cookie.

"Hey, how the hell did you get that
note inside a fortune cookie?"
I asked. Gunn laughed his
intoxicating laugh,

"Now, that would be telling,
Frankie."

"But..."

"Magic!"
I smiled.

"Abra-ka-fucking-dabra."

"Yeah, Frank, Abra-ka-fucking-
dabra."
He wiped a long strand of black shiny
hair away from his face.

"Like, the tavern, why is it now

derelict? Another one of your magic tricks?"

"Do you not know the rule of magic, kid? A magician never gives up his secrets. If he did, he would be cast out, he would have nothing and the magic would die."
I thought on it for a moment,

"I guess."

My hands were beginning to twitch. I pulled out a cigarette from my pack and lit it up. Calder noticed my hands.

"How's the writing going?"

"I can't stop and I am exhausted. Did you do this to me?"
Calder grinned, ignoring my question.

"That's what I like to hear, you should suffer for your art, Frankie. Without suffering, there is no reward."

"But...you tricked me. I'm not in control of my hands, they have a mind of their own now."

"Look, Frank, I gave you everything you wanted, you should be happy."

"I just..."

"Just nothing. I gave you things you could only dream of. I gave you back the power to write, I saved your liver, I gave you a dazzling smile. You should be grateful, you look like a pre-pubescent kid with an amazing writing career ahead of you."

The truth is, in the beginning it was wonderful, writing again, I mean. I felt alive, like I have never felt before. The downside was the fact that it was not me writing. The thoughts were not mine and it felt as though I was being pulled around like a puppet. It was almost as though I had no control over my hands and my thoughts any more – I was a prisoner in my own body. And to be fair, Gunn never told me what I was in for, otherwise I would have kindly refused his 'help'.

I decided to cut to the chase,

"So, why the meeting tonight, Mr Gunn?"

He rubbed his chin. I noticed then that he no longer had finger nails and it looked as though he had a serious fungal infection.

"I need your help, Frankie my boy."

Gunn started to unbutton his shirt. I was dreading to think what kind of help he was looking for.

"What kind of help?"

Gunn, pulled open his shirt, releasing the most putrid smell I have ever experienced; it was like a combination of sour milk and six-month-old rat shit - although, I'm no odour expert.

There was a massive hole in his stomach, it was the size of a basketball and went all the way through; I could have put my hand through his stomach and out through his back without touching the sides. It looked as though it was burnt around the edges and was covered in congealed blood which looked black.

I was sick in my mouth. I managed to swallow it back down quickly.

Calder had no insides left and yet he was still standing there. That is when I really began to question who or *what* he was. He may have resembled a human, but I am telling you right now, he was not.

"What the fuck happened to you? You look as though you have been shot repeatedly in the guts with a double-barrel shotgun!"

"Trust me, Frankie, I would take the double-barrel over this decay any day."

"What-"

"This is why I need your help. You

need to help me fix this. If I don't
fix this tonight, I will be gone by
sunrise."

"In case you hadn't noticed, Gunn,
you gave me the power to write again,
not the power of a fucking surgeon."

"You owe me, and if you don't give
me what I'm owed, you too will perish
in the very moment I depart from this
world."

"You mean I will die when you do?"

"In a sense."

"What the hell does that mean?"

"You drank the venom, Frank. By
doing so, you entered into an
agreement with me. You have to fulfil
your side of the deal and then you
will be free again."

This was too much for my mind to
process and I began to feel faint.

"What is it that you want me to
do?"

"You have to kill for me, Frank! I

need to feed. If you choose not to do this, we both die."

"Kill? You want me to commit fucking murder for you? You are insane!"

I tried to leave at that point. But Gunn raised his hand and pointed at me. There was a screeching noise and then, no matter how hard I tried to walk away, I couldn't.

"I'm not sure about you, Frank, but I like it here. I'm sure you are not ready to die. Think of your writing, the fame that awaits you."

"Infamous is what you mean. I will rot in prison!"

"Would it make a difference if I told you there is no way anyone will find out? Just our little secret, Frank." ·

"You *are* insane! The police always find out."

"You are wrong, Frank, and I am

rather insulted at your lack of faith in me."

"Someone will find the body sooner or later!"

"What if there was no body?"

"I'm confused."

"You shouldn't underestimate me, dear Frank. You have not yet seen what I am capable of."

I didn't want to think about it. I wanted to be the alcoholic, chain-smoking, manic depressive old bastard I was before I met Calder Gunn.

"So, just to get this straight, you want me to run up to some random old fella and kill him in cold blood? If I do, I will be free, if I don't, I die?"

"Yes, although it cannot be a random attack on just anyone, it has to be someone you know."

This was getting more and more fucked up by the minute. But I believed every single word I was hearing, and I honestly thought I would die if I didn't do what he said.

"I don't know anyone who deserves to die, unfortunately."

"Oh, but you do Frank."

"Who?"

"He will be here soon, then you will see."

"So you picked someone for me?"

"That's how it works, Frank."

"I'm not doing it! I will do anything you want, but not that!"

"The thing is, Frank, I like you. But if you don't do it, I will rip your fucking heart out of your chest!"

His voice was a roar. He was going to bloody kill me.

I wish I had read the small print when I was entering into this horrible nightmare. I was about to

become a murderer because I thought I
had to or I would die. It was
surreal. And who would believe my
story? There are no words to describe
how sick I felt about the whole
thing. And it only got worse.

Even if I decided not to do what he
asked, he would kill me. Either way,
I was royally fucked.

My eyes instantly filled up with
tears when I met my victim, for I did
know him. He was all alone and in the
dark – literally. Gunn had it all
worked out from the start. He preyed
on me because I was weak. Now I had
to kill a weak man.

Before I met my victim and
committed the horrible act, Gunn gave
me precise instructions on how to do
it. From his inside jacket pocket, he
produced a small dagger; it looked
ancient and I reckon it would have
better served a glass cabinet in an

ancient history museum.

Calder placed the dagger in my hand and I reluctantly gripped it. I felt a surge of heat pass through my body. I knew what was going on, I could see, hear, breathe and move, but I was no longer me. I was under Gunn's spell.

"You have to get him right in the heart, Frank. You cannot miss. Push the dagger in hard and pull it out fast."

I could not believe what I was about to do. Gunn was controlling me and there was nothing I could do about it. He was going to get what he wanted, regardless.

"What if I miss?"

"Unfortunately, if you miss, we die."

I sighed. I was shaking all over, and I was scared I would miss the heart. I didn't even know at the time if I had the balls to do it.

"It is time,"
Gunn said, raising his hand and pointing to the entrance of the alley.

For a moment I could not see anything more than the shape of someone approaching in the darkness. The closer the person got, I could make out a man. And when he was about twenty feet away I could make out exactly who it was.

Remember old Johnny from the AA meetings? The guy who lost his Linda? Well he was going to be my victim in just a few moments. He looked happy to see me and that made me feel as sad as hell. I was about to plunge him in the heart with a fucking dagger.

I held the dagger behind my back to hide it from him.

"Frank?"

He sounded confused,

"what in the heck are you doing here?"

I couldn't answer the poor old bastard. He was still rocking double-denim, it made me feel sorry for him. I thought about his life. Where did he come from? Why was he so weak? Why did he think it was acceptable to roam the streets wearing double-denim?

I can still feel the warmth from the single tear that streamed down my left cheek, just before I plugged him.

"I'M SORRY!"

Johnny looked baffled as hell at first, but, as I unleashed the knife from behind my back, the cold look of sudden realisation on his poor face almost made me die on the spot. I can still hear his voice at night sometimes in my dreams, screaming my name,

"FRANK!"

I could feel the bones in his chest crunch as I forced the blade into his heart, it was a direct hit. The wind escaped from his open mouth, he said nothing more, though he started gargling and his eyes bulged. Blood streamed from the corners of his mouth and he clutched at his chest.

He fell to the ground with a thud. And that was the end of him. He no longer looked like a person. He looked like a doll. I wished at that moment I would wake up in my bed and realise it was all a sickening dream - I didn't. This was a sickening reality.

I turned and looked at Gunn. He was laughing and clapping his hands,

"Bravo, Frank, Bravo!"

I snapped out of his spell. I was dazed for a moment and then I spewed up my guts. I wanted to cut the bastard's throat and shit down his neck.

"Look what you made me do! Are you happy now?"

"I am ecstatic!" He exclaimed.

That is when he began to change and showed himself to me for who he really was.

His eyes turned a reddish-orange colour. Blue veins became visible and began to pulsate all over his face. I could only stand there and watch, I had no words, and I also began to fear for my own life.

Gunn opened his mouth wide, releasing an almighty howl. His teeth were no longer white. They had turned yellow and were now crooked and jaggy. Long brown nails grew from his fingers. I could not believe this was happening right in front of me, I almost fainted, though I think I was too terrified to do even that.

Gunn pounced on the lifeless body in front of us. He placed his mouth around Johnny's and began to suck out his very soul, I swear to God. His body was almost transparent, and I could see a bright white light enter him.

When Gunn was finished sucking out whatever life remained inside Johnny, his body began to regenerate, right in front my eyes. The hole in his stomach began to fix itself, his skin and teeth became flawless once again. He buttoned himself up as though nothing had happened.

"What the fuck did you just do?" I screamed.

"I am not of this earth. I have, how shall I put it, certain needs."

"You are telling me you *need* to suck people dry?"

"Yes. You need food and water, I need...this to survive. I'm not like you, Frank."

I considered these words for a moment. I wished he was full of shit, but I had witnessed it, which made it hard to deny.

"This is fucked up!"

"Needs, must. All I can do is thank you for your sacrifice. I didn't think you had it in you."

I began to panic.

"Now what do we do with the body?"

"Simple,"

He replied calmly, walking over to the body which now looked like a dried up prune. He stomped on it, and that was it. The corpse crumbled like ash, into nothing, as though Johnny had never existed. Gunn gave me a wicked stare, I feared I was next.

I was astonished at what I just witnessed.

"What now?"

"Now it is over."

"That's it? No more murder?"

I was still holding the dagger, blood dripping from the edge. I looked down at it and a sudden surge of shame fell over me.

"You never can tell, Frankie my boy."

I knew it. I would be his puppet for the rest of my life. He would take control of me and use me whenever he wanted. I felt dead inside. Gunn tipped his hat towards me, and began to walk away, into the night.

"But-"
He turned to face me.

"You should be proud. You were weak like your father. I made you strong."
My stomach sank at the mention of my father.

"My father was a good man! What the

hell do you know?"

"Your father was a worthless drunk and you know it. I tried to help him, Frank, sadly it never turned out the way we planned. You see, he never had the balls to commit murder!"

"You didn't know my father, you are full of shit!"

"I know he came to me and made a deal. He wanted to make sure you were successful, and you were, were you not? *Heaven From Below*, ring any bells in that stupid head of yours?"

He *did* know my father.

"My success was down to you? No wonder my life has been such a misery."

"He didn't keep his side of the deal, so he had to die. Your success sadly died with him."

A rage built up inside me like never before. My hand was gripping the dagger so hard it ached. I

pounced at Gunn, raising the knife
into the air and repeating the
stabbing action I used to take out
old Johnny. But, as the knife came
speeding down, it met nothing but
air. Gunn was gone. A few moments
later, I heard his growl, it was
faint and then disappeared into the
night.

I sat in the shower for hours that
night with the door locked, scared to
move and constantly scrubbing my
hands. The whole night felt like a
dream and I began to wonder if I had
really killed a man. I was no killer,
was I? I would never be the same
again, I mean, how would I know I was
me and not under Gunn's spell?

The heat of the shower started to
make me feel nauseous and dizzy and
when I stood I began to sway. The

world started to turn fuzzy and I thought it was the onset of a migraine, as once again everything turned white. The sound of the shower pierced my brain as though a million needles were being forced through the organ in my head. And then it went black.

9

"Frank? Frank, are you okay?"

I came round. The voice was sweet,
music to my ears. I opened my eyes. I
was lying flat on my back. Sarah was
looking down on me, into my eyes. I
was so happy to see her beautiful
face, she was concerned. I sat up and
looked around. I was at an AA
meeting, I don't know how the hell I
got there, but I did.

"What happened?"
I asked.

"You fell right out of the damn
chair. Did you bang your head?"
The back of my head was aching.

"I guess so."
Sarah sighed with relief.

"Let's get you up."

She helped me to my feet, I staggered for a few seconds and then I steadied up.

"I'm sorry. I've not been feeling myself lately."

Sarah stared into my eyes with a look of confusion on her face, and the next words she spoke made me shiver from head to toe,

"You look different, too."
I ran my hands over my face,

"I just had a shave, that's all."

She looked mystified. I doubt she was convinced, but it would have to do.

"Take a seat and I'll fetch you a glass of-"

"No, it's okay, really. I just need to go home and get some sleep."

I looked around to see If Johnny was sitting there. He wasn't. His seat was empty. I missed his annoying voice already.

I staggered out into the street, a breeze caressed my skin. The sky was clear and the stars looked amazing. I walked home slowly, taking it all in.

I felt as though I had woken from a ten-year-long coma. Nothing seemed real to me, it was as though I was a zombie, the walking-fucking-dead. I thought about Johnny all the way home, questioning myself if I had really murdered him, it felt like a distant memory. What had Gunn done to me? To my mind?

10

The banging on my front door was horrible. A sharp tingling sensation shot through my ears. Opening my eyes was a struggle. I thought if I lay there long enough, the caller at the door would give up and fuck off.

Five minutes passed, the banging was so unbearable on my sensitive skull; I crawled out of bed and made my way down the hallway to the door.

"I'm coming, I'm coming!" I called.

I fumbled around the keyhole for a few moments before finally managing to open the front door. The light stung my eyes as it burst into the hallway without mercy.

"Mr Denver?"

A deep male voice questioned.

As my eyes adjusted I could see there were two men on my doorstep. I nearly shit my pants on the spot when I realised it was the Pigs.

"Yeah, I'm Mr Denver, what's the problem?"

I was sure they knew everything and I was also sure they could see through my bullshit. My only comfort if I was arrested for the murder was the fact that I would get life imprisonment, which also meant life safe from Gunn.

One of the guys was tall, thin and bald. The other was smaller and fatter with greying hair. The tall guy took the lead,

"I am Detective Inspector Hanley," Hanley pointed to his smaller sidekick,

"and this is Detective Stevens. May

we come inside?"

Guilt spills itself in fear of being spilled.

"Certainly, what's the problem?" I asked, ushering the suits into my house. I could feel myself beginning to sweat.

We walked down the hallway and into the lounge.

"Mr Denver, I think you should take a seat," said Stevens.

Are they always this nice and calm towards murderers?

"Okay."

I sat on my chair. I was now very curious as to what the fuck was going on. Why were these two little piggies standing in my lounge, treating me like a true gent?

"Just to clarify, you are Mr Francis Denver?"

"That's right."

The rest was a blur. The only words

I could make out were these,

"Mr Denver, your mother was involved in an accident yesterday evening. I am very sorry to inform you that she died at the scene."

I crumbled inside. I fell to my knees, I cried like a five year old boy, hiding behind his mother's skirt.

All this time, I had never contacted her, she had never contacted me, and now, in that moment, I would have given anything just to hear her voice again, to hear her saying my name.

Karma kills.

11

Time passed, though nothing was ever
the same for me. My hands still
trembled and when they did, no matter
how hard I tried to resist it, I had
to write. And, as promised, I sold
many paperback books, and I guess you
could say I found a little fame.
There was no glory in this for me, I
was forever cold inside.

I've not aged a day since I met
Calder Gunn, and I have a funny
feeling that he won't let me. I am
cursed. Now and then I still hear him
whispering to me in my dreams and no
matter how hard I try, I can't block
him out.

I think about my mother and my
father every night before I go to

bed, and every morning when I wake up, and I am not afraid to admit that I miss them dearly.

I had committed murder and my soul would be forever tainted. Now and then I also think about Johnny. I think about what he would be doing? I find comfort in telling myself he would have died from liver failure anyway. This may have been the case, but who was I to decide another man's fate? Nobody, that's who. I will have to live with what I have done for the rest of my life.

So, if you are ever down on your luck, and a man with a black suit, green tie and a trilby hat offers to help you, don't sip on the venom from his flask. Instead, turn around and run away as fast as you can and never look back.

Two weeks ago I sat down to write,
and there on my desk, wrapped ever so
prettily, was a parcel. I had seen
this before and I knew what was
waiting for me inside.

My passion became my burden.

Frank Denver.

END

RANCID: THE CRYSTAL MAN

COMING SOON

RANCID

CONTACT:

grantjollywriter@hotmail.co.uk

www.facebook.com/GrantJollyWriter

4759813R00072

Printed in Great Britain
by Amazon.co.uk, Ltd.,
Marston Gate.